Monk

Written by Jill Eggleton
Illustrated by Philip Webb

The monkeys could see the bulldozers . . .

. . . big, yellow bulldozers.

The monkeys didn't like bulldozers coming into **their** jungle. They stayed very still in the trees.

The bulldozers stopped and the men got off.

"We'll have lunch here," said Matt.

4

"Look at this grass," said Mike.
"I won't sit on it.
We'll have to get
a log to sit on."

Matt and Mike put their lunch down and went to get a log.

The monkeys came down from the trees . . .

. . . **creep, creep, creep.**

They snatched the lunch . . .

. . . and back they went, up the trees again.

Then **plonk** . . . down came an apple on Matt's head, and . . .

plonk . . . down came an orange on Mike's head.

Matt and Mike looked up the tree.
"Monkeys," said Matt.
"No lunch for us today."

Matt and Mike sat down
on the log.
But it was very hot and
they went to sleep.

The monkeys came down
from the trees and sat
on the bulldozers.

When Matt and Mike woke up, they saw the monkeys on the bulldozers.

"**Get off!**" shouted Matt. "Go back to your trees!"

But the monkeys stayed
on the bulldozers.

"Let's go," said Matt.
"We'll come back
when it's dark.
The monkeys will be gone."

When Matt and Mike came back, the monkeys were in the trees.

But at the top of a tall, tall tree were the keys for the bulldozers!

A Story Sequence

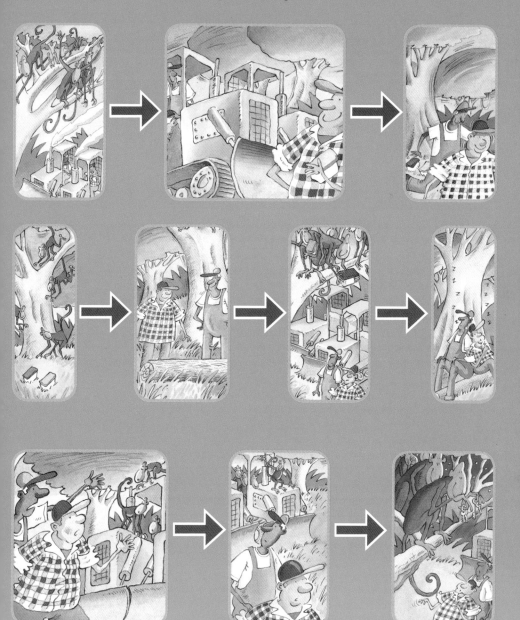

Guide Notes

Title: **Monkey Watch**
Stage: Early (4) – Green

Genre: Fiction
Approach: Guided Reading
Processes: Thinking Critically, Exploring Language, Processing Information
Written and Visual Focus: Story Sequence, Speech Bubbles

THINKING CRITICALLY
(sample questions)
- What do you think this story could be about? Look at the title and discuss.
- Look at the cover. What do you think the monkey's could be pointing at?
- Look at pages 2 and 3. Why do you think the monkeys didn't want bulldozers in their jungle?
- Look at page 5. Why do you think Mike didn't want to sit on the long grass?
- Look at pages 6 and 7. Why do you think the monkeys took their lunch?
- Look at page 11. Why do you think the monkeys sat on the bulldozers?
- Look at page 13. Why do you think Mike and Matt knew the monkeys would be gone if they went back to the bulldozers when it was dark?
- Look at page 14. How do you think Mike and Matt could get the keys back?

EXPLORING LANGUAGE

Terminology
Title, cover, illustrations, author, illustrator

Vocabulary
Interest words: keys, watch, jungle, snatched, creep, log, plonk, bulldozers
High-frequency words: still, won't, gone, could
Positional words: on, into, off, down, in, up
Compound word: bulldozer

Print Conventions
Capital letter for sentence beginnings and names (**M**ike, **M**att), periods, commas, exclamation marks, quotation marks, question mark, ellipses, possessive apostrophes